A Path of Stars

Anne Sibley O'Brien

MAINE
HUMANITIES
COUNCIL

Charlesbridge

Last winter, before the phone call came, my Lok Yeay, my grandmother, would tell me stories.

"When I was a girl in Cambodia," she said, "living in the house by the river, we grew lemongrass, just like this." She pointed to the stalk she was chopping for our sour soup. I took a carrot from the pile for my baby brother, Kiri, to chew on.

"All around the house were trees, full of coconuts, mangoes, and oranges," Lok Yeay said as the soup simmered. "The air smelled of flowers—hibiscus and roses. Oh, Dara, the air was so sweet." Lok Yeay smiled, her eyes shining like stars. The rice bubbled in the cooker. The steam jiggled the lid open, closed, open, closed, chattering a story as warm and happy as Lok Yeay's.

At dinner, we ate the soup and laughed at Kiri's messy face. My grandmother's story went on. "In the evenings I sat with my brother, your Lok Ta, in the coconut tree. We would pick and share a sweet mango, its juice dripping down our chins. We sat there for hours, listening to the crickets as the moon rose. Then we would play hide-and-seek in the moon's light with our brothers and sisters, our cousins, and our friends."

From the photograph on the wall, Lok Ta's smiling eyes looked as if he, too, were remembering.

In the early spring, before the phone call came, Lok Yeay told more stories as I helped her cook for Cambodian New Year.

"When I was a girl in Cambodia," she said, "we went to the temple, a real temple, not just a house like here in America. But we ate these same foods, just the way my mother taught me to make them."

I helped Lok Yeay serve the feast at the temple. Everyone loved her chicken curry and her rice cakes in banana leaves. People wore their most beautiful clothing and sat on the floor before the monk, listening and praying.

As we rode home, our breath making mist in the cold air, Lok Yeay pointed at the dark sky.

"In America it is so cold that the stars glitter like diamonds," she said. "But in Cambodia, the air is so soft and warm that the stars glow like fireflies.

"At night our family gathered on the wooden platform in the yard. Our father built a fire on the ground to smoke away mosquitoes. And what do you think we did, sitting under the sky, all together?" She knew I loved this part of the story. "We watched the stars!"

I couldn't help smiling, because my name, Dara, means "star." Lok Yeay was the one who had named me.

"The grandparents would point to the sky and show us the Chicken with all her baby chicks," Lok Yeay told me, "and the long line of stars called the Crocodile. My brother kept asking questions, wanting to learn all he could about the stars. But the rest of us fell asleep, listening to star stories."

I smiled and pointed to Kiri, sound asleep in his car seat.

Later in the spring, before the phone call came, Lok Yeay watched me and Kiri after school. "When your mother was just a baby, as small as your brother is now," Lok Yeay said, "there was a day the birds stopped singing, a day the soldiers came." She sat still, and her hands stopped sewing. She didn't see me or my brother. She was deep inside, inside a sad, sad story.

After a time, she raised her head and began again. "Four years later, we ran from the war. By then I had only two people left—my brother, who is your Lok Ta, and my little daughter, who is your mother. We took turns carrying her on our back, just the way you are carrying your brother.

"Lok Ta and I held on to the only treasures we had been able to save: your mother, and pictures of those who had died. So many people—our parents, our brothers and sisters, my husband, Lok Ta's wife.

"We hid in the jungle by day and walked at night by the light of the stars. Lok Ta read the stars like a map, finding our way west. We prayed so hard to the Buddha, *Pre Ang, please help us,* and we asked our lost family to guide us. Their spirits brought us to the border of Thailand, where we found safety at a camp."

This summer, before the phone call came, she told another story. "In the camp we had gardens where we grew vegetables, squash like that." She pointed to a bright green zucchini. "But no flowers. Oh, Dara, how we missed the flowers.

"It was so crowded and so noisy in the camp. But we had a small space in a long house, your mother, Lok Ta, and I. We made a tiny altar for the Buddha, and put the pictures of our family next to it, to remember them in our prayers."

She watched as I rolled a ball to my brother. "Your mother was happy to be with other children. It was the first time in her life that it was safe to play."

I helped Lok Yeay and my mother gather vegetables from our garden, peppers, tomatoes, green beans, spinach, and onions. As we carried the baskets home, Lok Yeay said, "When your mother was a girl, she and I came to America, to Maine, in the cold winter. But Lok Ta went back to Cambodia, hoping to find anyone still alive from our family. He went back to the house by the river. He found some of our cousins. He married a new wife and made a home there. Someday I will take you to Cambodia to meet Lok Ta and his family."

That's how Lok Yeay's stories ended, every time.
I imagined flying to Cambodia on a big silver plane,
seeing the house by the river, and meeting Lok Ta
and his family.

Then last week, just as the autumn air was turning cool, the phone call came. My cousins, calling from Cambodia, told Lok Yeay that Lok Ta had died.

All the light went out of Lok Yeay's eyes. She slipped like a whisper into her bed. She wouldn't speak, and she wouldn't get up, no matter what Mama did.

The house is silent now. The kitchen is empty and quiet and dark. The rice in the cooker is cold. Tonight when Papa came home from work, he brought takeout from the Thai restaurant. When Mama took her a plate, Lok Yeay wouldn't eat a bite.

Lok Ta died, but it seems as if he took Lok Yeay with him, too.

Out in the garden, I look up at the stars and say a prayer. *Pre Ang, please help me. I don't know what to do.* And I say a prayer to Lok Ta. *Help Lok Yeay.*

The breeze stirs the leaves of the plants. My eyes spot a pale, perfect rosebud, shining in the starlight. I think of how much Lok Yeay loves roses. Nearby, one large tomato hangs heavy on the vine. I pick them both.

I step into the still, dark kitchen and flip the light switch. I get a chair to stand on, then run water into a jar for the rose. I get a tray from the counter and spoon some rice into a small bowl. It is cold, but maybe Lok Yeay will eat some. I put the rice, the tomato, the rose, and two spoons on the tray.

In the living room, Mama helps me take the photograph of Lok Ta off the wall. I add it to the tray.

"Lok Yeay," I call from the doorway. "It's me,
Dara." My voice is unsteady. Lok Yeay doesn't
answer. The tray is heavy, so I push the door
open and slip into the dark, silent room.

I put the tray down on the bed and
climb up beside it. Lok Yeay stirs and
turns. She looks at me with flat, dull eyes.
Lok Ta, please help me.

I hold out the yellow rose.

Lok Yeay's hand comes up, slowly, and
takes the flower.

"Lok Yeay," I say, "can we say a prayer for
Lok Ta?" She looks at me for a long time, as if
she's coming back from far, far away. She nods.

I take Lok Yeay's hand and guide her to the living room. We take the photograph of Lok Ta and put it on the wall in our shrine. We place the rose on the shelf next to the statue of the Buddha and light the incense for our prayer. Sitting before the shrine, we pray for the spirit of Lok Ta, that he may find peace.

I climb back on the bed with Lok Yeay, to share cold rice and bites of fresh tomato. Its juice drips down our chins.

"Lok Yeay," I say, "I will tell you a story.

"Someday, you and I and Mama and Papa and Kiri will all go back to visit Cambodia. We will fly on a big silver plane, through the sky, through the stars. We will find the house by the river and our family living there. We will pick mangoes from the tree and eat them. All around us, the air will smell of flowers."

Lok Yeay curves her hand along my cheek.
"My Dara," she says. "My star."

Author's Note

When the Maine Humanities Council commissioned me to create a picture book representing Maine's Cambodian American community, I knew that my own experiences and perspective weren't sufficient to tell an authentic story. But if I immersed myself enough in the experiences of contemporary Cambodian people, perhaps such a story might come through me.

I started by reading every survivor memoir I could find, until the outline of life in Cambodia before 1975, the Killing Fields, the escape, and life in a new land became familiar. I talked with several scholars about trauma survival and the sociology of Cambodian Americans. Most significantly, I listened to my friends Veasna and Peng Kem, who spent hours sharing their own memories with me. Many of the details in this story come from their accounts, or were inspired by them.

Filled up with these stories of Cambodia's beauty, culture, and people, and their harrowing trauma, unspeakable loss, and heroic survival, I waited. Many weeks later, a story began to take form, beginning with the image of a girl in a garden picking a tomato and a rose.

I used many reference photos for visual details, especially the portraits in Kari René Hall's *Beyond the Killing Fields*, a photo-essay of refugees in a Thai-Cambodian border camp in the late 1980s. My art was created with oil paints on gessoed paper, with accents in water-soluble oil crayon.

I look forward to seeing many more children's books about the Cambodian experience told by new generations of Cambodian Americans themselves.

History of Cambodians in Maine

In 1975 soldiers of the Khmer Rouge marched into the cities of Cambodia, which they called Kampuchea, and force-marched its citizens into the country for farm labor and reeducation. Over the next four years, nearly two million Cambodians died by execution, overwork, or starvation.

Among survivors, hundreds of thousands fled, mostly on foot, to refugee camps in Thailand and Vietnam. From 1975 to 1999, when the last border camp was closed, nearly one hundred fifty thousand Cambodian refugees were admitted to the United States. In the late 1970s some of these families began to move to Maine, most from the area of Battambang. Once Cambodia's government was stabilized, some who came to the United States as refugees chose to return to their homeland, to search for missing family, or to contribute their skills to rebuild the country. Today about two thousand five hundred Cambodians live in Maine.

Note from Pirun Sen, Cambodian American educator and founder of Watt Samaki Temple, Inc.

I want readers of this story to understand the value of the relationship between the grandparent and the grandchild. That has been a Cambodian tradition going back thousands of years, the base of our culture. In my own case, I spent less time with my parents because they were working. I spent more time with my grandmother, who was the one who told me stories, taught me, disciplined me. Whether she was going to the temple ceremony or a wedding party, she would drag the grandchildren along. Right now, I miss my grandmother more than my parents.

I want the reader to see that connection, and I want to keep that tradition, to build strong relationships between the generations. Due to the environment, we cannot do that here in the United States. Children spend social time outside the home with their peers instead of with their grandparents. The grandparents do not value themselves as much as a resource for stories from Cambodia. There are too many options here that drag them away from each other. One starts to walk to the right, one to the left. So the string is stretched and stretched and sometimes it breaks. We need to keep trying to build that personal bond.

About the Maine Humanities Council

A *Path of Stars* was originally developed for the New Mainers Book Project, part of the Maine Humanities Council's Born to Read program. The project sponsors high-quality children's picture books created from the experiences of Maine's refugee communities, to preserve and present their cultural heritage and to promote their English-language literacy.

The Maine Humanities Council—a statewide nonprofit organization—enriches the lives of people in Maine through literature, history, philosophy, and culture. Its programs, events, grants, and online resources encourage critical thinking and conversation across social, economic, and cultural boundries. Visit MHC at **http://mainehumanities.org**.

Glossary

Dara (dah-rah)—a name meaning "star"

Kiri (kee-ree)—a name meaning "mountain"

Lok Ta (loak tah)—grandfather, or any older male relative. In this story, Lok Ta is Dara's great-uncle, her grandmother's brother.

Lok Yeay (loak yay)—grandmother, or any older female relative

Pre Ang (preh awng)—a term meaning "Lord" or "Excellency," used to address the Buddha, God, a king, or other respected authority

Acknowledgments

Many thanks to Denise Pendleton and the Maine Humanities Council for trusting me with this project.

To Jan L. Thompson of the University of Southern Maine for her help in understanding the psychology of trauma and how it plays out over generations.

To Julie G. Canniff for sharing her study of the adjustment of Cambodian families in Maine.

To the crew at Charlesbridge, especially Whitney Leader-Picone, Emily Mitchell, Yolanda Scott, and Susan Sherman. I couldn't have done it without you.

To Pirun Sen, for carefully reviewing the final draft of the book and for his helpful suggestions in making it more authentic.

Most of all, to Veasna and Peng Kem for their generosity in sharing their stories and their ongoing guidance as I developed this book over many years.

Published by Charlesbridge
85 Main Street
Watertown, MA 02472
(617) 926-0329
www.charlesbridge.com

Library of Congress Cataloging-in-Publication Data
O'Brien, Anne Sibley.
   A path of stars / Anne Sibley O'Brien ; in association with
the Maine Humanities Council.
      p. cm.
   Summary: A refugee from Cambodia, Dara's beloved grandmother is grief-stricken when she learns her brother has died, and it is up to Dara to try and heal her.
   ISBN: 978-1-57091-735-6 (reinforced for library use)
   ISBN: 978-1-60734-079-9 (ebook pdf)
1. Cambodian Americans—Juvenile fiction. 2. Refugees—Cambodia—Juvenile fiction.
3. Grandmothers—Juvenile fiction. 4. Granddaughters—Juvenile fiction. 5. Grief—Juvenile fiction.
6. Bereavement—Juvenile fiction. 7. Maine—Juvenile fiction. [1. Cambodian Americans—Fiction.
2. Refugees—Fiction. 3. Grandmothers—Fiction. 4. Grief—Fiction. 5. Maine—Fiction.
6. Cambodia—Fiction.] I. Maine Humanities Council. II. Title.
PZ7.O1267Pat 2012
813.54—dc22   2011003472

Printed in China
(hc) 10 9 8 7 6 5 4 3 2

Illustrations done in oil paint and water soluble oil crayon on paper
Display type and text type set in P22 Tai Chi and Sabon
Color separations by KHL Chroma Graphics, Singapore
Printed by Imago in China
Production supervision by Brian G. Walker
Designed by Whitney Leader-Picone